Space Shuttle Blasts Off!

Peter Bently

Illustrated by Louise Conway

Space Shuttle is on the **launch pad** at the **Space Centre**.

The **tank** and **rocket boosters** are full of **fuel**.

"We're going to collect a **broken satellite**," says Commander Mandy.

When the **astronauts** are strapped in, the ground crew locks the shuttle door. In the control room, the **countdown** begins.

The astronauts do their last checks. Everything is working fine.

"All systems go!" says Commander Mandy. "Prepare for lift-off!"

Ten-nine-eight...

Commander Mandy starts the main engines.

Seven-six-five-four...

"Maximum power!" shouts Commander Mandy.
Three-two-one...

Roar!

"Lift off!"

With a terrific blast, Space Shuttle rises from the launch pad.

Space Shuttle soars **higher** and **higher**.
Soon it is high above the **ocean**.

"Release the rocket boosters!"
shouts Commander Mandy.

"Check!" says Co-pilot Andy, flipping a switch.

The empty **rocket boosters** fall away.

They **splash** down into the sea.

A **ship** is waiting to collect them.

The crew can see the **Earth** below as Space Shuttle **flies** into **space**.

"**Release the fuel tank!**"
orders Commander Mandy.

Clunk!

"**Check!**" says Co-pilot Andy.

The empty fuel tank **burns up** as it **tumbles** back to the Earth.

Commander Mandy **steers** Space Shuttle into **orbit** around the Earth.

"Look, that must be the **broken satellite!**" says Co-pilot Andy.

Space Shuttle **moves** into position below the satellite. Commander Mandy **opens** the **cargo doors.**

Co-pilot Andy moves a **joystick** to control the **robot arm.**

Whirr!

"Carefully does it," says Commander Mandy.

The arm grips the **satellite** and pulls it into the **cargo bay.**

"What a **weird** satellite!" says Commander Mandy.

The **crew** prepare to close the cargo doors.
Suddenly, they hear a **strange** sound.

Knock!
Knock!

"Maybe the cargo doors are stuck," says Commander Mandy. "I'll go outside and look. It's spacewalk time!"

Commander Mandy puts on her space suit and helmet. The shuttle door opens and she floats out into space.

She comes face to face with - an **alien!**

"You've got my **spaceship!**" says the alien.

"Let us go or my children will be late for school on **Mars!**"

"**Whoops, sorry!**" says Commander Mandy. "We thought you were a satellite!"

Space Shuttle releases the alien spaceship.
"Thanks Earthlings," says the alien.
"Next stop Mars!"

Zooom!

The spaceship
flies off.

The astronauts soon spot the **real** broken **satellite**. They load it into the cargo bay...

...and close the **cargo doors. Click!**

"Mission accomplished!" says Commander Mandy.

Space Shuttle glides back down to earth. It **lands** with a gentle **bump** and rolls to a halt.

The **crew transporter** collects the crew.

Hold on - **who is that?**

It's a stowaway
alien!

"**Space Shuttle** is
more **fun** than school!"
she squeaks.

"**Uh-oh!**" sighs
Commander Mandy.

"Space Shuttle to
blast off again!"

Let's look at
Space Shuttle

Rudder
(Vertical flap on tail)

Main engines

Elevons
(flaps on wings)

Delta wings

Rocket boosters

Vertical stabilizer (tail)

Cargo doors

Cargo bay

Crew module
(flight deck)

Fuel tank

Other Space Vehicles

Shuttle Carrier Aircraft

Crawler-transporter

Fuel tank transporter

Crew transporter

For Clyst St Mary
Primary School, Devon P.B.

For Gavin - your support
means the world L.C.

Quarto is the authority on a wide range of topics.

Quarto educates, entertains and enriches the lives of our readers—enthusiasts and lovers of hands-on living.

www.quartoknows.com

Designer: Verity Clark
Art Director: Laura Roberts-Jensen
Editors: Tasha Percy and Sophie Hallam
Editorial Director: Victoria Garrard

Copyright © QED Publishing 2016

First published in hardback in the UK in 2015 by QED Publishing
Part of The Quarto Group
The Old Brewery, 6 Blundell Street, London, N7 9BH

A catalogue record for this book is available from the British Library.

ISBN 978 1 78493 117 9

Printed in China